BROOPS! DOWN THE CHIMNEY

A spacechild comes down to Earth with a bump in this hilarious story!

Nicholas Fisk has had a number of different occupations. He's served in the RAF, been an actor, a book editor, a jazz musician, a journalist, and worked in advertising. He's now a highly successful author particularly well-known for his science fiction stories. Nicholas Fisk is married with four children and lives in Hertfordshire.

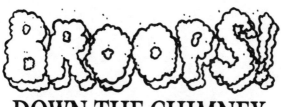

DOWN THE CHIMNEY

Nicholas Fisk

Illustrations by
Russell Ayto

WALKER BOOKS
AND SUBSIDIARIES

LONDON • BOSTON • SYDNEY

First published 1991 by Walker Books Ltd
87 Vauxhall Walk, London SE11 5HJ

This edition published 1997

4 6 8 10 9 7 5

Printed in England by Clays Ltd, St Ives plc

British Library Cataloguing in Publication Data
A catalogue record for this book is available
from the British Library.

ISBN 0-7445-5288-5

CONTENTS

Down the Chimney

Our house is old enough to have a chimney for coal fires and sometimes we have a proper fire, but only in the living room. When Broops fell out of his spaceship, he came down our chimney.

I was the only one awake. I had a Call of Nature in the middle of the night. Just when I was about to flush the loo, I heard a funny tumbling noise.

I ran to where it came from – the living room – and there was Broops. I could hardly see him for the cloud of soot. I said, "Good gosh!" and he said, "Broops."

I asked him who he was and he said

"Broops" again, which wasn't much help. So I asked him what he was and he put one of his fingers – he's got fingers – into his pudding-y tum and wiggled it. He has a gadget inside him that lets him understand and talk all kinds of languages.

He got the wrong language to start with and said something like "M'yester porkwee scurdle omsk." He told me later that's how they talk on Ipsilon 3, second on the left when you pass Venus. I said, "I beg your pardon?" and he had another wiggle and said, "Oh, sorry. I am a friendly alien from another planet."

I said, "I suppose you want me to take you to my leader?" and he said, "No, whatever you do, don't do that. I'll get into all sorts of trouble. Just hide me away. And anyhow, what is that stuff about leaders?"

I explained that bug-eyed aliens from space always say, "Take me to your leader!" That's the first thing a Martian would say – I've seen it in the comics.

He said, "You don't take me for a Martian? Martians are rotten." He was really offended.

So I asked him where he was from and he told me, but I must never reveal the place or tell anyone his proper name. He made me promise. I can't even tell my sister Polly.

Well, I wouldn't, would I? She's only five and no good at keeping secrets. She rushes around squeaking, "I've got a SECRET!" and as soon as you ask her what it is she tells you. I mean, really!

In any case, I can't pronounce the alien's name, it sounds like a drain being cleared. I called him Broops because that is one of his special sounds.

I asked him why he had picked our chimney to fall down and he said that he hadn't, he just happened to be there.

He'd been messing about, disobeying his parents, and he fell out of the spaceship.

The same sort of thing happens to me – I fell out of the oak tree, on to the garage roof and bust my collar bone.

Most of the time Broops is very fat, but he can change his shape. He made himself long and narrow to come down the chimney and he hasn't got a collar bone to bust. I don't know if he has any bones at all. Lots of creatures don't. They are Invertebrates.

"You've made an awful mess; all this soot," I said. "Mum will be furious." Really, it wasn't that bad – soot is all right if you don't touch it.

Broops said, "It is a windy night, couldn't this stuff just have blown down?" I had not thought of that. Broops thinks of all sorts of things that you and I might never think of and that was one of them.

I replied, "Hmm, ymm, you have a point there," which is what Twerpy Tombs is always saying. He puts the tips of his fingers together and looks at the ceiling when he says it. It is his way of avoiding responsibility. He's our Relief Teacher. They must be scraping the barrel to come up with someone like Twerpy Tombs.

I didn't know what to do with Broops. When I said, "I may have to tell Mum about you," he gave a "Breep!" like a kitten being squeezed and started on again about being kept secret, and how he was the representative of a pure and clean race, so contact with other races would spoil everything.

"You don't look very pure and noble sitting in a lot of soot," I said. He pretended not to hear.

He put out some fingers and pulled at my pyjamas and asked, "Is that *you*?" I said, "What do you mean?"

"Is that your skin?"

"No, of course not! These are just my pyjamas."

"Breep?"

"Pyjamas. The clothes you wear at night."

"Clothes?"

"Don't be so dim, everyone wears clothes! Summer clothes, winter clothes, uniforms, the lot!"

At this moment the cat-flap rattled and old Sooky waddled in. Broops said, "Who is *that*?"

"That's Sooky, our cat." I stroked Sooky's forehead and said, "Who's a lovely boy, then?"

"I like his clothes," Broops said. "They fit him so well. Not like yours, all baggy."

"That's not *clothes*, that's *fur*! It's part of him. All part of the service when he's born."

"But you told me everyone wears clothes."

"When I said everyone, I didn't mean animals." Then I had to explain about the birds and bees and butterflies and badgers not needing clothes. I must admit I got rather mixed up.

"You are sounding stupid," Broops said when I dried up. "You look stupid, too, in those clothes of yours. Why, even your eyes have got clothes on!"

"Those are my specs," I told him. "Just forget about them, right?" I happen not to like people making funny remarks about my specs, calling me "Goggles" and all that. My name is James, thank you very much. But you can call me Jamie or Jay if you like.

Broops gave a soothing "Brooo-ooops", meaning "Sorry", and started preening his fur, which he is very proud of. It's all very well for him (or she, or it – I never found out if Broops is male, female or middlesex) because he's got really good fur, all soft and silky, cream on his tum and lots of gold and brown everywhere else. No specs, no pyjamas. But I musn't tell anyone too much about him, I promised not to, remember?

* * *

I went to the door to let Sooky go to his bed. On the way I trod on one of Polly's Noah's Ark animals. "Ow!" I said, and hopped about. "Ow, ow, ow, where're my slippers?" I found them and put them on to protect my feet.

"Breeps!" said Broops, in amazement. "What are those?"

"Slippers, of course. For my feet."

"You mean, even your feet wear clothes?"

"Well, it stands to reason," I began to say, but Broops started his wheezy, breepy, squeaky, hooty laugh. I like his laugh, I've even learned to imitate it. But just then I was fed up so I threw a slipper at him.

It missed, of course. That's a weird thing about Broops. He can not only change shape, but place. When you think he is fat, he goes thin. When you think he is standing over there, he can be somewhere else.

It comes in handy, obviously. I mean, that's how he got down our chimney. And when it comes to having a fight … but I'll tell you about that later.

Pollysister

When I threw the slipper at Broops, it knocked over my tin robot which is heavy with dud batteries. It made an awful clatter when it fell down. Broops laughed again and I said, "Sssh! You'll wake Polly!"

"What's Polly?" Broops said.

"My sister. She's only five, so she's a bit barmy. She can't help it."

"Let me see Pollysister!"

"Not Pollysister, she's not a plastic. She's a human, like me."

We stood over the sleeping Polly, looking down at her dark curly hair on the pillow.

"There, you've seen her," I said. "Let's go, she's fast asleep."

Polly, without even opening one eye, said, "Oh no, I'm not!" and sat bolt upright in bed. "M'yah, fooled you!" she said.

The dawn was just about breaking outside, so there was enough light for her to see Broops. "What's that?" she squeaked, very loudly. "Can I have it?"

"It's Broops. Keep quiet. I'll explain."

"He's lovely! Is he for me? I want him."

When she said this, Broops gave a soppy sort of broopsy-whoopsy sound and his fat face went all smirky. But by the time she had finished saying it, she had fallen back on her pillow and was fast asleep again.

Broops said, "I like the Pollysister, I really do!" He added, "She's better than you."

When dawn had properly finished breaking and it was morning, I said, "I'm hungry, I must have breakfast."

"Breakfast?" said Broops.

"It's a meal. Food. You eat it."

"What does Pollysister eat?"

"Oh, sausages, bacon, cornflakes, toast … anything she can get her greedy little hands on."

"I'll have what Pollysister has."

"It's not Pollysister, I've told you. Just Polly. You make her sound like – like wallpaper paste."

I wished I had never said it. Breakfast was forgotten. Broops had to know all about wallpaper and rooms and houses and villages and towns. I had to answer three million questions. While I told him things, he opened all the packs and bottles and shelves in the kitchen. He was a whizz at undoing things. I tried to keep an eye on him, but he was always somewhere else spilling treacle, flour, chutney, Brasso and I don't know what else on the floor. Guess who had to clean it all up? Right first time.

Dad was in Holland or somewhere and Mum had been rushing about, and now she had gone in her usual panic. I slapped Polly's breakfast on the table – she was still sleeping – then got out the vacuum cleaner and cleared up all the soot. I was glad to have half an hour to myself before Mum came back.

Broops kept asking crazy questions – "Does a vacuum cleaner clean vacuums?" stuff like that – and I got angrier and angrier with him. Yet I liked him more and more.

I told him about families, and he said it was much the same on his planet. He soon understood about Polly being my sister and all that. He liked Polly.

"Where is she?" he demanded.

"She'll be down in a moment."

"Good. Where are your parents? Are they your leaders?"

"Yes, I suppose so. They boss us about."

"Then they're leaders," Broops said. "The same as on our planet. They tell you what to do all the time. They think they know best…

You have to obey them."

"But clever old you, you disobeyed!" I said. "And you ended up falling down our chimney. Ha ha ha!"

"Oh, tush put!" Broops answered. "Just tush put!"

"It's not 'tush put', it's 'shut up'. So boo-sucks and no returns."

I thought I had won this round, but I hadn't. "What are boo-sucks?" Broops wanted to know. "Are they good? Does Polly have them?"

"Oh, tush put!" I said.

I looked at the clock and said, "Ouch! I'll be late for school! I've got to get moving!"

"School?" Broops said. "We have school, too! School, I go to school every day, how I love it! The dear old school…!"

I said something about him being mad, school was awful, but Broops did not hear, he kept on saying, "School, broops! School, lovely!"

"Polly won't be there," I told him. "She's too young."

"Never mind, I'll tell her all about our thrilling day when we return from school!" Broops said.

"Anyhow, you can't come. Even old Twerpy Tombs would notice an extra bod when he does the register," I said. But then I thought, perhaps he won't. My pal Fatty Foster won't be there, he's ill. Broops could take his place, sitting next to me. He would have to be disguised of course. But how?

We talked about various ways. Broops came up with the best idea. He said, "I'll wear clothes, that is what I'll do! Clothes, all over me!"

I began to tell him that wouldn't do, his fat furry face would still be visible, but then I had a brilliant idea. I said, "You've got a cold, an awful cold, see? A cold in the head. You can't speak properly, you can only splutter. And you're completely wrapped up!"

He did not know about colds. I had to

teach him how to splutter, cough, sniffle and wheeze. He did it very well, I must say. I gave him a huge scarf that hid most of his head and lots of tissues to bury his face and nose. Then I stuck my father's grotty old school cap on top of everything.

"Go on," I said, "let's hear you sneeze and wheeze. And keep wiping your nose. That's it, great, one more time!"

"I'll do anything you say," he wheezed.

"Anything at all, as long as it gets me to your beautiful school!"

Dear Old School

It is seven minutes' fast walk to my school. Usually I do it in eight and get told off in front of the class for being late again. As we hurried along, I warned Broops about Twerpy Tombs, our teacher (some people call him Moosejaw – his face sort of sags into his chest). "He's a real berk," I told Broops.

"Oh, I'm sure he is! How nice!"

"And he sometimes gets sarky," I said.

"Sarky? Oh good, I like sarks. We sark and sark like anything at my school!" Broops said.

It was useless telling him things. His mind was made up. He did not want to be confused by the facts.

"What blessing will we be having?" he asked.

"They're not *blessings*, they're *lessons*."

"Same thing," Broops said. "What will our tutors tute us?"

I gave him the full horror story of maths, geography, history, binary maths and all the rest of it. Then I said, "Just remember three things. The first and most important is, you've got such a bad cold that you can hardly speak. So if anyone speaks to you, just do the coughing and sneezing bit."

"What are the other two things?" he asked.

"William the Conqueror, ten sixty-six," I said desperately. "And twice two are four, twice three are six, twice four are eight." I thought, This will drive me bonkers!

He spent the last minutes of our walk repeating the things I taught him. "William the Conqueror, twice three is four," he muttered happily. "Twice four is bonkers. Am I saying it right?"

"Great, fine, terrific," I groaned.

*   *   *

I sat Broops next to me in Fatty's usual place and old Twerpy arrived, all dirty trainers and designer stubble. He called the register.

When he got to Fatty's name, I nudged Broops and he said, "Breep!" and Twerpy Tombs looked up. Quick as anything I explained. "Please, sir, Fatty's got a cold, sir, he can't talk properly, sir!" and Twerpy looked down again and got on with ticking off names. Phew...!

Twerpy Tombs started us off on Mental Arithmetic. He really believes in it. He thinks it is evil to use calculators for all our sums; we should be able to do them in our heads. Fat chance. We hide our calculators in our laps.

"Hmm, ymm," he began. "We are in the supermarket. We buy three packs of eating pears, at ninety pence a pack. How much, someone?"

"Ooh, sir, two pounds seventy pence!" piped Jennifer Mincing, first as usual.

At this moment, Broops had to chip in. "William the Conqueror!" he said.

"I beg your pardon?" said Twerpy.

"William pears, sir!" I said. "They are the juiciest! Fatty's favourite, William pears!"

"You have a point there," Twerpy said. "Hmm. Ymm. Now we will purchase three bunches of bananas at one pound fifteen each, and four packs of cornflakes…" And so it went on and on, till at last he said, "Right! What is our grand total, anyone?"

Naturally Jennifer's nice clean hand was the first to go up. But before she could say anything, Broops said, "*Ten sixty-six!*" I could have murdered him.

But old Twerpy said, "Not bad, not bad at all! Very close! Now, Jennifer, give us the correct answer."

"Ooh, sir, ten pounds eighty-five pence pree-cisely!" said the little prig, smirking her head off. She was right, of course. She always is. She got a return smirk from old Twerpy.

And Broops got out of trouble. For the time being.

* * *

When break-time came, I seized Broops by one of his scarves and said, "Listen, you goof! Keep your mouth shut! Don't say another word!"

He started saying something about school being better on his planet, but I said, "Just shut up and keep out of trouble." And for a time he did.

But then Jennifer, her long, blonde, freshly-shampooed hair flying, cycled past us. Twerpy Tombs had sent her on a Special Mission, posting his letters. To the betting shop, no doubt.

Broops seemed astonished. "What is she *doing*?" he squeaked.

"Riding her bike inside school grounds," I replied bitterly. "*We*'re not allowed to. But if you are teacher's pet —"

"No, what is she *doing*?"

"Riding her crummy bike," I said, beginning to understand. He had never seen a person on a bike.

"Crummybike…!" he almost whispered.
"But it's impossible! Why doesn't she fall off?
Her crummybike has only two wheels!"

"That's usual with bikes," I said.

Broops hardly heard. His gobstopper eyes
were fixed on the fast disappearing figure of
Jennifer. "She's brilliant!" he said. "She defies
all natural laws! This is the most amazing
sight your planet has to offer!"

Well, I suppose it is a bit marvellous to
whizz along on only two wheels, with
nothing sticking out at the sides to support
you. Obviously they had never learned the
trick on Broops' planet.

"Do you own a crummybike?" he said.

"*Bike*, it's just *bike*. Yes, I own one."
I didn't tell him how crummy my bike is,
it would only start confusing things all
over again.

"Can you ride it?"

"Yes, of course! I mean, you don't have
bikes just to stick on the mantelpiece like
ornaments!"

"Do animals have bikes?"

I said no, not even Sooky. I didn't tell him
about bears riding bikes, or chimpanzees.
Confusion again.

"I must ride your bike!" Broops burst out
passionately.

"Oh no, you mustn't."

"I must! I will!" Broops cried, clasping his
fat hands (if they are hands) over his heart
(I suppose he has a heart).

"I must ride your bike!" he said. And that
very evening he did. That is how the rear-
brake lever got bashed up.

Hanglebars

"Listen, Broops, you podgy moron," I said that evening, "I'm not going to let you do it!"

"He's not a moron, he's my best friend!" Polly said, throwing her arms round Broops. "What is a moron?" she added.

"A moron is someone who wants to ride a bike when he doesn't know how," I said.

"Don't mind *him*, Broops," Polly said. "He's just a *brother*. Come with me, Broops, I'll take you to the bike. It's round the back, I'll show you!" There is no stopping Polly. I trailed after them.

We took Broops and the bike to the concrete path by the playground. Nobody goes there any more since the skateboarders lost interest.

It was getting quite dark. I stood there saying nothing and feeling pessimistic while Polly got on with the bicycle-riding lesson.

"You just sit on the saggle," she said, "and hold tight to the hanglebars. Then you peggle. See?"

Next moment, he was peggling – I mean pedalling – and she was shouting, "Yes! Yes!"

Polly beamed, I scowled and Broops fell off.

It is no use asking me how many times he fell off, I soon lost count. Most of the time he fell on to the grass. That didn't matter because the bike was not hurt. But then he came off on the concrete and that was serious: the rear-brake lever was bent, really badly.

"Isn't he lovely?" was all Polly said. "And so brave! Oh, he's fallen off again. Well, never mind, he's ever so bunjy. Peggle, Broops! Peggle faster!"

Finally Broops went right over the handlebars, on to his head. It looked awful, but there were no metallic noises from the bike so I did not worry too much.

Polly, of course, was worried only about Broops. "Oh, poor thing!" she hooted. "Are you hurting dreadful? Are there any bomes broken?" She can't even say "bones" properly.

Broops was quite all right, just a bit stunned. While I examined the bike, Polly cradled him in her arms and started singing him a lullaby, if you please! To make him feel better! Fat chance, her voice is like a dentist's drill.

This is what she sang...

"WOCK-a-bye Broopsy
ON a twee top
WHEN the bough breaks
Poor Broopsy go BOP."

If you had someone squeaking this drivel in your ear you'd go mad, wouldn't you? So how do you think Broops took it? What did he think of it?

I'll tell you. He loved it. He rocked in rhythm. He went all droopy and fubsy. "Please," he begged Polly. "Please do it again!"

She did it again. It set my teeth on edge. But Broops said, "Oh, give me more of it! What is it?"

"What is what?" Polly said.

"That thing you are doing from your mouth."

"That is singing," Polly said. "Beautiful music. Don't you have music where you come from?"

"Do some more! Don't ever stop!"

So there we were in the dark and cold, with Polly singing, if you call that singing, and Broops dreamily waving one arm keeping time, and my poor old bike quite forgotten. Except by me.

Polly knows about a million songs, worse luck. Grandpa teaches her. He knows every song there ever was if it is rude: the sort of songs soldiers sing in the back of army trucks.

He is a terrible old man, disgusting. Mum dreads his visits. He wears one of those caps like a bun, and stained cardigans with the buttons done up wrong. Polly thinks he is terrific and he dotes on her. He is always giving her Mars bars. I never get any.

"Sing another one!" Broops said. "No, do the last one again, the sad one about the thin baby." So Polly started all over again...

A mother was bathing her baby one night,
T'was the youngest of ten and a delicate mite.
The mother was poor and the baby was thin,
It was only a skellington wrapped up in skin.
The mother looked round for the
*   soap on the rack,*
T'was only a moment, but when
*   she looked back –*
Her baby was GONE! *And in anguish,*
*   she cried,*
"Oh, where is my baby?" The angels replied,
"Your baby has gone down the plug'ole!
Your baby has gone down the plug!
The poor little things was so
*   skinny and thin,*
It oughter bin washed in a jug."

"Don't stop, go on!" Broops cried. "This is the sad part, isn't it?"

Polly went on and on. Broops' eyes were misty with grief. Soon he started crying. I had not known that he had tear glands, but he certainly had. He wept buckets.

He wept even when she sang the song that goes: *There were rats, rats, big as bloomin' cats, in the Quartermaster's stores.* He cried his eyes out over the chorus that goes: *My eyes are dim, I cannot see, I have not got my specs with me.*

He cheered up a bit when Polly sang *We are the Ovaltineys*, but grew sad again when told that he could not be an Ovaltiney, they finished years ago. He said, "What were they? Were they superhumans?" and Polly said no, she didn't think so, did I know?

I said, "I'll never get this brake-lever right again. If you want to know about stupid Ovaltiney, ask ghastly Grandpa."

I knew if you did ask him, he'd only say, "Hah! Got you puzzled, eh? Well, I'm off to the boozer!"

It was an awful evening.

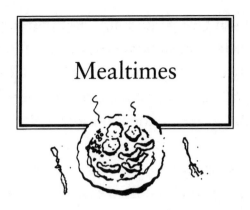

Mealtimes

It's a good thing I've got my tape-recorder. I'd go mad if I had to write all this down. How do writers do it? Why? The money, I suppose, but Fatty's father is a writer and he has only got an old Volvo.

It's all right with the recorder, you just gabble away at it. I suppose I've done a million words already and I am not at all tired.

And anyhow, the whole Broops story took just a few days, then suddenly finished.

If it had gone on longer, Mum would have found out about our secret visitor. She didn't, though, because she is always rushing about doing things. Useful things, nothing stupid. We hardly see her some weeks. She flings food at us, rushes about laughing and then the front door slams and her Mini goes "Grrr … grrr … grrr…" and at last the Mini starts and she's off again.

This does not mean she is uncaring. She is great at the weekends. We go all over the place in the Mini. I wouldn't swap her for anyone, not even a Royal's mum, but the Royals do have smashing cars. Dad says, "Why don't you let me buy you a proper car?" but she loves her Mini, body-filler and all.

Dad gets grim about mending the Mini whenever he is home, but that isn't often because he is some sort of consulting engineer. He is always off to Brussels or somewhere. Once he went to Japan. Mum says he is a workaholic and he says, "Would you rather have an alcoholic?"

All this explains why we were able to keep Broops secret. Well, it partly explains it. The other thing to remember is, *Broops could change shape.* So when Mum or Dad were about, and likely to burst in on us at any moment, we only had to say, "Roly-poly, Broops" – and he'd curl himself into a blob for Polly to sit on, or for me to rest my back against.

There's always so much clutter in our home that you'd never notice another bit of "furniture". Not unless you happened to spot Broops' eyes peeping out from all that fur. But he soon learned to keep his eyes closed if Mum came in. And Dad never notices anything, he just bumbles about looking for his specs and humming to himself. You'd like our dad.

So hiding Broops was not all that worrying. What did worry me was, How do you feed him? What does he eat?

"Do that again!" Broops said, when, for the first time, he saw us noshing. "Wheep!" he said. "Vreep! That's brilliant!"

Polly and I did not know what he meant.

I asked him what was puzzling him.

"Where's it gone?" he said. "How do you make it vanish? What is it?"

It was the food on our forks or spoons. As you know, you fork or spoon food to your mouth; chomp at it; swallow it, then start again, making another mouthful do its disappearing act.

"It's vanished!" Broops said. "Oh, what a clever trick! Where has it gone?"

Polly said, "Down the lickle red lane, past the lamppost and down into his hey-fatty-tum-tum. Hee hee."

It went on like that for quite a time. Polly being silly and me trying to explain about human digestion. Broops just could not get the idea at all, so I said, "Oh come *on*, you have food on your planet, haven't you?"

"Well, yes, but we do not eat anything," he said. "The food is just … *there*, in the air. You live and breathe and that takes care of eating, too."

"That can't be true!" Polly said. "It would be so boring! I couldn't live without sausages and cream and choclick and hamburglars." (She couldn't, either. She's a terrific pig.)

I said, "But Broops, aren't you hungry? You haven't eaten for yonks! Not since you've been here on Earth."

"Oh, I can always change shape," he said. "You know, get a bit thinner or eat up some of my own fat. There must be Earth creatures that can do the same thing."

He was right, when you come to think of it. Some sea creatures don't really *eat*, they just filter sea water through their cake-holes and keep all the nourishing bits inside them as food. Oh, and earthworms, they're the same, only they do it with earth.

"Never mind about food, do some shape-changing!" Polly ordered. So he did, just to please her. One minute he was fat and round,

another minute like a furry crocodile. Polly beamed and clapped. I thought how handy it must be, being able to change shape whenever you wanted.

Thumping Thugsy

On the very next day, I saw just how handy it was.

There was a boy at our school called Thugsy Thurlow. He is about the oldest boy in the school, which isn't very old, but you should see Thugsy! He is twice the size of anyone else and twenty times as nasty. He's got spiky hair, great sweaty red hands and bovver boots. His hobby is hitting smaller people as hard and as often as he finds convenient. He has not actually killed anyone yet, but "Give him time, give him time", as Mr Tombs says.

We were on our way home from school

when suddenly the sky darkened and Thugsy loomed over us, blocking out the sun.

"Wanna fight?" he said. "Smash your face in if you like." All conversations with Thugsy start like that.

I said, "No, thank you very much. And anyhow, you can't hit me, I'm wearing spectacles."

"Smash the specs in first," Thugsy suggested, "then your face." He grinned greenly at me. He should brush those fangs of his one day.

"No, thank you very much," I said again and tried to worm my way past. Thugsy detained me by seizing my throat and choking me.

"Wassamatter with this one?" Thugsy said, still strangling me but looking at Broops. "Well wrapped up, aren't you? Gotta nasty cold, have you?" (Broops, of course, was all covered in woolly things.) "Sneeze and snivel, do you?" Thugsy said to him. "Right then – go on, let's hear you snivel." As he spoke, he used a spare hand to punch Broops right where his nose should have been.

Broops said, "Vreep!" and fell over backwards. You tend to do that when Thugsy punches you. Thugsy said, "Here, on your feet, stand to attention! I want you to stand up like a little soldier, so I can knock you down again."

The worst thing anyone can do in these circumstances is to stand up. Broops did it. He got to his feet. "Ooops. Ooops! Breep!" he said. "I think I know how you do that. But show me again."

"Don't mind," Thugsy said and knocked Broops down, as before. Thugsy must have a very good eye, he landed Broops in exactly the same place on the ground.

"Ooh!" Broops said. Then he started making those high, wheezy breeps and vreeps that he does when he is laughing. Laughing! After being hit by Thugsy!

I helped Broops up. "I know what we're doing," he told me. "This is a fight!"

"More like a murder," I said. "Let's get away!" But Broops said, "Thugsy fights nicely. Please may I play too?"

I said, "Are you mad?" and Thugsy said much the same thing, but with some adjectives thrown in.

Again Broops started breeping and veeping, as if laughing – then all of a sudden he changed shape! He stretched himself higher than a lamppost! He shot up so fast that his scarves and things flew out sideways, I saw furry bits of Broops in the gaps. Thugsy gaped and so did I.

The very top part of Broops became a fat ball. He looked like a lollipop on its stick. It took a split second to do all this.

Then – down came the big, bunjy lollipop right on Thugsy's head. The noise it made was BOOOMPF! The top half of Thugsy disappeared into the lollipop. But not before I caught a glimpse of Thugsy's eyes. They were completely circular, like this –

All lovely and innocent, like a newborn babe's when it sits on its nappy pin.

His mouth was circular, too.

"Am I doing it right?" Broops asked me. By now, he was bouncing himself up and down on Thugsy's head: Boompf! boompf! boompf! "Is this the right way to fight?"

"It will do," I said.

"Where I come from, we call this Physical Training," Broops explained. "We keep this up for hours," (boompf!) "and hours," (boompf!) "and hours." (boompf!)

"I think perhaps you should stop soon," I said to him. "Thugsy might be getting a little tired."

"*I'm* not tired at all!" Broops said, boompfing away harder than ever until the heels of Thugsy's bovver boots rattled on the pavement.

All the same, Broops must have got tired because eventually he stopped, panting a bit while he adjusted his scarves and hat. Thugsy just sat there on the pavement, eyes crossed and face scarlet, feebly moving his arms and legs like a drunk bumblebee.

"I do like your friend Thugsy!" Broops said to me. "He is nice to play with."

Thugsy managed a groan, but only a little one.

"We'll play again tomorrow, yes?" Broops said to him.

Thugsy said, "Oh, you beastly bully, boo hoo!" and did some weeping.

He was quite all right at school from then on. No more thumpings.

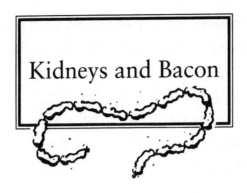

Kidneys and Bacon

You must not think that Broops was a tough guy just because he gave Thugsy such a going-over. Broops wasn't, not at all. At heart he was just a great big jellybaby with fur on.

Look what happened that time we walked back from school the long way round. We did this because Mum told me to collect the sausages for supper from Mr Thompson the butcher.

"Don't forget, now!" she had said.

"No, Mum, I won't. I'll tie a knot in my neck to remind me."

"I'll tie it for you!" she had said, chasing me round the kitchen. We had a good giggle.

So Broops and I returned home the long way, past the shops. All the time, Broops peered out of the scarves and things hiding his furry head. He took everything in.

"What's that?" he said, when three pigeons took off at our feet, not wanting to be trodden on. They flapped like anything, the way pigeons do.

"They're pigeons," I told Broops. "Birds."

"But they are not the same as the other birds you showed me," Broops said. "They're bigger. They're huge! Are they bird-monsters?"

"No, just … pigeons," I said.

"What are they *for*?" Broops wanted to know.

"They're not for anything. They're just there, like sparrows and blackbirds and starlings."

"They must be for something," Broops said.

"Well, yes, I suppose you're right. There are racing pigeons, and carrier pigeons carrying messages, and homing pigeons, and pigeons in pies."

"Pies?" Broops said. "Why would pigeons want to live in pies?"

"They don't *live* in them, they're *put* in them. To be eaten."

As I spoke, I remembered that Mum once gave us a pigeon pie. Only once. It wasn't very good, hardly any taste to it. Thinking about that pie, I hardly noticed that Broops had stopped walking. He was just standing there, goggle-eyed.

"*Eaten*?" he said. "You don't mean – you can't mean – that *people* eat *pigeons*?"

"Never mind all that," I said. "Here we are at the butcher's. I've got to pick up some sausages."

Broops, still protesting, followed me into the shop. "But you couldn't! – you wouldn't! – eat a poor, feathery *bird*!" he said. "It would choke you!"

"You take the feathers off first," I explained. "We only eat the meaty bits."

Broops ran out of words, he could only breep and broop. And I was busy talking to Mr Thompson, who said, "Ah, sausages for your ma. Where did I put them? They must be in the back, yes, there they are."

While this went on, Broops was looking at all the carcases hanging from hooks, and the lumps of beef and mutton ready to be cut up, and the trays of livers and kidneys. I was gazing at the kidneys. Even when raw, they make my mouth water. There's nothing like kidneys and bacon.

Then I noticed that Broops was sort of staggering about, saying, "Broop-broop … but you can't … breep… but you wouldn't, you couldn't…!"

I said, "What are you on about?"

"You don't! You can't!" Broops said. He began to reel and stagger. I grabbed him and the sausages, and got them out of the shop as quickly as possible. Outside on the pavement he fell about worse than ever, but at least fewer people saw him. I hate scenes.

"What's the matter?" I hissed.

"Those… (broops!)… things in the …(breep!)… shop," he said, "were *live animals*!"

"Dead animals," I corrected him. "We don't eat live animals, it's not nice."

"But they were alive *once*," Broops said.

"Yes, of course, what are you getting at? Pigs become pork, sheep become mutton, beef comes from cows or bulls, I forget which."

"*Sausages!*" Broops gasped. "What are sausages made from?"

"That's anybody's guess," I said. "They're a bit of a mystery, sausages. All I know is, my favourite sausages are —"

Broops never got to hear about my favourite sausages because he fell flat on his back – *plomp!* – on the pavement. Just like that, plomp! He had fainted. Falling did not hurt him. He was too fat and furry to damage himself. But it was an awful job getting him upright and walking. All the way home he kept nagging me about how HORRIBLE we are to eat animals, that we must be mad.

All I could do was agree with him. It got a bit boring, having to keep saying, "Yes, you're right, I do agree with you," and all that. I cheered myself up by squeezing the nice packet of sausages I carried. Sausages, tomatoes and mash! You can't beat it.

No, hang on. Kidneys and bacon are even better.

Alien Bites Dog

Did I tell you, earlier on, that Broops seemed to like my little sister Polly more than me? Yes, I did. He even said, "She's better than you!" which I thought was cheek.

But it wasn't cheek, not really. It was because of her size. She is only little. Broops never liked big humans, I think they frightened him. Polly was just about his size, though of course Broops was a million times fatter. You can't really compare Broops and Polly any more than you can compare a teddy bear and a doll. Not that it matters.

What did matter was he and Polly were about the same mental age. Broops recognized this straight away, from the moment he saw her asleep in bed. I think Broops could pick up vibes, he could *feel* something radiating from people. He liked what he felt from her – a sort of loony quality, the kind of barminess you see in puppies and kittens and children of Polly's age. Polly is as mad as a hatter.

At Christmas, she came roaring in on everyone saying, "I ARREST you, oh yes, I do. I am the great DETECTIVE, I have handcuffs." She did have handcuffs, too, toy ones from Taiwan or somewhere. Also a rotten magnifying glass and one of those Sherlock Holmes hats. Uncle Ron gave her the stuff. Anyhow, she arrested Uncle Ron and handcuffed him very tightly. Then it turned out that the release-catch thing would not work and Uncle Ron's wrists began swelling and going red (so did his face), and in the end the cuffs had to be hacksawn off. Lots of blood and bad language.

When it was all over, guess what Polly did?

She burst into tears – she can cry louder than anyone – and shouted, "My PRISONER, you've let him ESCAPE! And he's a MURDERER!"

You can't reason with people like that, they are loonies. And Broops was a loony of the Polly sort. Yes, I know he could speak our language, and pick things up quick as anything, but that wasn't *Broops*, it was the stuff they implanted in him. His equipment. I don't know what gadgets and things they use, but I do know that the real Broops was just about Polly's age.

I mean, take the business about the dog bite. You would not have done it, I would not have done it. But Polly might, and Broops actually *did*.

Miss Fremlin at number forty-seven, just down the road, has this dog. It is just the sort of dog you'd expect a very old lady to have – a cairn terrier or something like that, very small and hairy and low-slung and yappy.

Repulsive, really, but very old people are as barmy as very young people, I always think, and Miss Fremlin's dog is her sacred cow, if you know what I mean. She even uses a special voice to speak to it, a high-pitched whooping creak like a barn door closing.

When Broops was still dressed as a schoolboy – his head covered with scarves and the old cap perched on top – the dog caught sight of him and did not like what it saw. I don't blame the dog. Broops looked a real freak, but of course people always look the other way. Dogs don't. Miss Fremlin's dog rolled its horrible little eyes, went YAP-YAP-YAP, slipped its lead and fastened its tiny white teeth in Broops's left ankle.

Broops did not mind this at all. He just stared down at the dog's waggling body and listened to the "grr-grr" noises the dog was making; then he said, "Oh, a pussy cat."

"No," I said. "It's a dog. And it's biting you." I started pulling at the dog's lead, trying to be useful, but this never works.

Once a dog has got stuck in, you can't get it unstuck.

Miss Fremlin wasn't any use either. She just stood there saying, "Oh! You cruel, wicked boy! Leave poor Horatio alone!" What a name for a dog, Horatio…

Broops said, "Is it all right, the dog biting me?" he was not at all upset, just curious. The dog had no chance of getting through to anything that hurt – Broops's ankles are as furry as a polar bear's bottom.

I said, "No, it's *not* all right, it's all *wrong*. But what can I do about it?" I was pulling away like anything, and flapping my fists, and Miss Fremlin was flapping at me, and the dog was going "wurra-wurra-wurra" as it sank its stupid teeth deeper and deeper into Broops.

Then I said something I was to regret. "Come away, you little ratfink," I told the dog. "Leave go, or *I* will bite *you*!"

By now, Broops realized that something was wrong. He tried to walk away from the trouble, but the dog hung on and Broops could only go ninety-nine bonk, ninety-nine bonk, like a centipede with a wooden leg. Or a prisoner with a ball and chain round one ankle. Broops began to get cross.

"What does it mean, this biting?" he asked.

"It means the dog is angry with you."

"Well, I am angry with the dog."

"Yes, I see that. But this biting business only works one way. The dog bites you, but you can't bite back."

"Oh yes, I can," Broops said.

And he did.

You already know how Broops changed shape to thump Thugsy, our school bully. He did much the same thing now – that is, he sort of whooshed upwards then came down in an upside-down U. And then his jaws opened and closed and he bit the dog.

It must have been a really good bite because the dog made an extraordinary noise, like those hooters they had on old cars. Only much higher, as it was such a ratty little thing. Then – it all happened very quickly – it let go of Broops; Broops resumed his usual shape; and the dog streaked off to the safety of Miss Fremlin's loving arms. He really moved, he looked like a floor mop being catapulted by a huge rubber band.

He knocked Miss Fremlin over. She sat on the pavement with her legs sticking out while the dog tried to bury itself in the top half of her garments, and some people ran to help her up, and the dog yapped, and so did she, and so on and so on.

"Let's get out of this!" I snarled at Broops, and hauled him away by his scarves.

What I wanted, of course, was to find a place of safety – somewhere where no one could look at him too closely.

But even as I towed him along, I realized there was no such place. Several people had witnessed the Boy-bites-dog incident. Some must have taken a really good look at Broops, who never looked like a human boy at the best of times. I said sternly to myself, "This cannot go on! Think of something brilliant!"

The only brilliant thought that came to me was this: Broops' school days were over. They had to be. So Broops would have to stay at home, even though he would be left on his lonesome and would probably wreck everything in the house. Not a brilliant thought at all, you may say, and you would be right.

I talked it over with Polly. She wasn't much help. "It's your problem, oh yes, it is!" she said. "I am only a stupid little girl – you have often said so."

"Oh, come on, Polly," I said. "We've got to think of something to keep Broops amused and out of trouble. Try to be helpful."

"Don't want to help," she said. "You ate that slice of chocolate cake. *My* slice. The *very last* slice."

"Never mind that. This is serious —"

"I *do* mind. Chocolate cake is serious. And I'm going to watch telly and *m-yeah, m-yeah* to you!"

"Well, thank you very much!" I said to her retreating figure as she swept grandly from the room. (Grandly! – you must be joking! She'd got her skirt caught up in her knickers.)

But then, after a pause, I said, "Yes! Thank you very much!" all over again. Because she had given me the answer. Television.

Ruggles

Either we seem to watch telly all the time or not at all. When Broops came, a not-at-all time began: the TV set gathered dust.

As of now, however, whenever we were on our own, on went the telly – with Broops sitting in front of it.

"This is how you work it, Broops," I told him, showing him the remote control. "Press this button, and this, and this. Get it?"

He got it instantly, he was good at that sort of thing. But he said, "I want to go to school! Back to the dear old school, to play fighting with Thugsy, and everything!"

"Well, you can't," I told him. "Fatty has

got over his cold and he is back at school. So that's that. You stay here and watch telly."

"I don't want to!" he complained. "We do not have telly where I come from."

"What *do* you watch?"

"Flowers and things. Big flowers that sing and dance. I water them, often."

"Now you are going to watch TV, instead," I said. "It will make a nice change."

He stared at the TV set. "Does it sing and dance?" he said.

"Yes, sometimes. Often."

"Do I have to water it?"

"No, Broops. Never. Not ever. No water."

"Make it sing and dance."

I pressed the little buttons and various programmes came up on the screen, all of them dull. I looked anxiously at Broops's face and waited for him to complain.

But he didn't! His furry jaws gaped, his great big eyes were alight. "That man…!" he gasped.

"That man? He is a politician. He is making a party political broadcast. It will soon be over."

"That man…!" Broops said, not hearing me. "He's lovely! All furry, like me! Oh, what a beautiful, furry man!"

The party political man had a beard.

Broops liked TV more than anything in this world. He never got tired of watching it. When Polly and I came home, he told us about it.

"I saw the Queen," he said. "In a big gold thing with wheels. What is Queen?"

We explained about queens and kings.

"Can anyone be a queen or king? Can I

become king? Yes, I shall be king and Polly can be queen. And you … you can pull the big gold thing with wheels."

"Thank you," I said.

Polly giggled and said, "Better not let him pull it, Broops. He's not strong enough!"

"Thank you," I said.

The next day, the room was in a mess. Everything but the TV set was upside down.

"Broops! What is happened?" Polly said. She hurriedly started putting cushions back on chairs and straightening rugs and carpets.

"I've been playing ruggles," Broops said.

"Ruggles? What do you mean, ruggles?"

"Like this." Broops snatched a little round cushion from Polly and tore up and down the room with it. When a wall got in the way, he bounced off it. Often, he threw the little cushion at me or Polly. Sometimes he put it on the carpet, stared at it for a long time, then kicked it as hard as he could.

Frequently he fell over, very dramatically. Once he threw himself at me and knocked

both me and a chair over.

At last he stopped. "That's the end," he said. "I won."

"What do you mean, you won? Won what?"

"Ruggles," he said. "Like the telly."

Polly said, "Oh…! I get it!"

I said, "I don't."

"Rugger," Polly said. "He's been watching rugger."

"That's right, watching ruggles!" Broops said. "I won by ten-sixty-six."

"That's a big score for a rugger match," I said. "Who played against you?"

"Just me," said Broops.

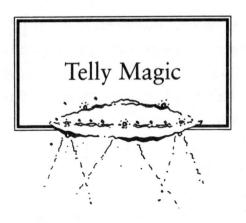

Telly Magic

Of course, this did not go on for ever, just for a few days. But it felt like for ever. We were very clever about hiding Broops – stuffing him under Polly's bed, or in the toy cupboard, or using him as a cushion – but sooner or later, someone would *see* something and *say* something and oh dear, oh dear, big trouble.

So I said to Broops, "Do you ever think of going home?"

Polly said to me, "Oh, how rude! Broops has only just come. And I've not had time to teach him more wriggles."

"Riddles," I said. "The word is riddles."

"That's what I said. Now, listen carefully,

Broops. Why is the desert like a snack bar?"

Poor old Broops was bored out of his mind with Polly's riddles, but he was always nice to her. "That is a very interesting riddle," he said, gravely nodding his enormous great woolly head.

"Well, go on then," Polly said. "What's the answer?"

"I will tell you, I really will," Broops said. "But first would you tell me what is a desert? And a snack bar?"

"Broops," I interrupted, "do you ever think of going home?"

But he did not hear me, Polly was bombing him with inaccurate information about snack bars and deserts.

"So the answer *is*," she ended up, "because of *all the sand which is there*. Sand-which-is, sandwiches is, get it?"

"Mmm, yes, of course," Broops said glumly.

"Brilliant, isn't it?" Polly said. "And I've got lots more. There's one about an elephant

and a gorilla, but I can't quite remember it –
give me time…"

"That's just what's worrying me, Broops,"
I said. "Time. You see, it's only a matter of
time before you are discovered. I mean, we
can't keep you hidden for ever —"

"Oh, but I thought I told you," Broops
said. "I'm going home tomorrow!"

"*Tomorrow?*" I said. Or sort of gasped.
Because I suddenly realized that although I
wanted to get shot of Broops, I didn't want
him actually to leave.

"Tomorrow, in the night," he said, plumply
and cosily. "It's all arranged."

Polly started howling and moaning about
him leaving. She said he musn't leave, he must

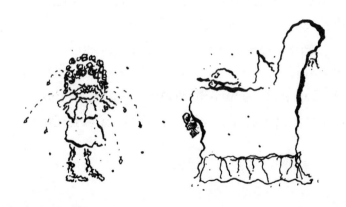

never leave, her heart would be broken, and all that.

Broops simply said, "I must go. They are picking me up."

"Who is picking you up?" I exploded. "How are they doing it? Who is they? How do you know about it?"

"Is that a riddle?" Broops asked. "It's a long one."

"Never mind riddles. How do you know you're being picked up?"

"The telly," Broops said. "They told me through the TV set. My people are picking me up tomorrow, at five o'clock in the morning, 05:00 Earth time."

"The *telly?*" I said. "But that's impossible!"

"The telly only shows programmes," Polly said. "You use the telephone for messages." She nodded her head wisely.

"My people use your telly," Broops explained. "But not during the programmes, of course. That would spoil the stories and things."

"Like the commercials," Polly said.

"But I like the commercials!" Broops started saying.

I interrupted him sharpish. "*How* did you get a *message* from your *people* on our *telly*?"

"The messages come through when you switch off," he told me. "You know how the screen goes dim for a second or two, then the light goes right out? Well, while it is going dim, that is when I get messages."

"That's impossible!" I said. And Polly said, "Yes, im-poss-ib-le!" Then she said, "Let's try it." She turned the TV set on, waited, then turned it off.

Nothing happened.

"There you are!" she crowed, and so did I. "Nothing!"

"Of course there is nothing!" Broops said. "My people have already said all they want to say.

And anyhow, the messages are probably invisible to you."

"But you still stand there —" I began.

"Sit there," Polly said.

"And tell me barefaced lies about the telly —"

"Furry-face lies," Polly said.

"Please!" Broops waved a woolly paw to silence us. "I am being collected, by the same ship that brought me, tomorrow at five o'clock, 05:00 hours. End of message."

"*Where* will they pick you up?" I asked.

"Here, of course. I will go the same way I came."

"The chimney?"

"The chimney. I don't want to stand outside in the cold, do I?"

"No, of course not! " Polly said. "And suppose it rained and your fur got all wet! And we weren't there to see you off! Oh, Broops, I don't want you to go!"

She went on and on about how she would miss him.

I just sat there thinking. What I thought was, I don't believe a word of what Broops has just told us.

Then I thought again. Suppose it *were* true! Suppose old Broops really was going to zoom up our chimney at the speed of light! Better still ... *suppose a socking great spaceship appeared in the night sky*!

I could just see it, and hear it. Terrific boomings and whinings and electronic noises; and lots of lights revolving in a massive saucer thing, and coloured rays belting downwards to hold it up...

The other things I could see and hear were, FAME! And UNTOLD WEALTH! Because I would sell the story, wouldn't I? I would alert the press, the TV people. I would manage the whole show. And what a show it would be! A real, genuine, super-de-luxe *spaceship, UFO, extra-terrestrial thingummy*, for the whole world to marvel at!

And at the centre of all the hoo-ha, rich and famous ME.

Rich and Famous

It did not work out as well as I had hoped.

I telephoned the big newspapers to give them the great news. I remember what one editor said: "Pull the other one, sonny, it's got bells on it."

The TV companies were just as bad. One TV lady was really insulting. "Gosh, darling, how thrilling!" she said. "A flying saucer, you say? A UFO? Well, of course I'm thrilled, who has ever heard of such a thing? *I* haven't, not more than three times a week. Oh, and sweetie-pops … *how old are you*?"

I thought this really gross – what has age to do with anything? So I rang off.

In the end, only a few people seemed to want to know about the spaceship. Our local policeman, PC Fuzz Farmiloe, said, "Spaceship, is it? Well, I don't mind keeping an eye on it – I'm on duty tomorrow night. Five o'clock, right? See you around." I could tell he was not really interested.

The trainee journalist on our local paper, *The Clarion*, also said she "didn't mind". She was going to some sort of rave-up that night, she might still be conscious at five.

I realized that it was all up to me. I got organized. I put a new tape in my tape recorder and got Dad to let me have our viddy camera. As usual he told me how careful I must be with it, and remember not to do this and that. It makes me laugh: when we use it, it is always me that has to explain to him how to work it. But never mind. I put film in our only good camera, the SLR with the wide-angle lens, and cleaned the viewfinder, which was filthy.

Next night, I set the alarm clock at

4.30 a.m.; promised Polly I would wake her up when things started happening; and went to bed fully dressed.

At 4.45 a.m. it was still very dark. Also wet and windy indoors, because Polly was blubbering and moaning and weeping as she clutched Broops, begging him not to go. He simply said, "I am very sorry but I must," and patted her head with his paw.

At 4.55 a.m. I crept out into the garden, loaded with all the film and tape gear.

PC Fuzz Farmiloe was there, surprise, surprise, grinning at me over the fence. "Any moment now, eh?" he said, then began making stupid spaceship noises.

Believe it or not, the journalist was out in the road too. She was with her boyfriend. They must have had a very good evening – they were both giggling and making corny jokes and pointing cameras at the sky.

They were not the only ones about. I never knew how many people are awake and doing

things in the night. There was even an old man on his way to his allotment. There must have been half a dozen people around when…

It all started.

A Sound in the Sky

4.59 a.m. A sound in the sky, a sound that got inside your head. And in the darkness, a lightness, a warm glow that sometimes flickered, then strengthened.

I ran indoors, outdoors, back and forth, like a headless chicken. I wanted to know what was happening in the sky; but just as much, I wanted to see Broops go up the chimney, if that was what was going to happen. And to wake Dad and Mum, but *did* I want to do that?

And the sound in the sky became louder and louder, the glow became a radiance, and the journalist kept saying, "I don't

believe it, I don't *believe* it!" and her
boyfriend's cigarette butt burned his fingers
and he swore like anything –

5.00 a.m. And it was *there*, over our house!
I saw it, it was there, low in the sky! Not a
saucer, nothing like that; more complicated
than a saucer, more like a living thing, some
sort of underwater creature – it changed
shape all the time. And no, it didn't have
portholes and a circle of lights, it had
darknesses here and there, like mouths or gills
opening. But it wasn't a dark thing, it was
luminous and a beautiful colour – no,
colours; various warm colours, but sometimes
there were violet stripes running across it.

It was big and bright and beautiful and
changing. And it was just the right size for the
viddy and film cameras. It filled the
viewfinders – I couldn't go wrong. I just had
to keep pressing buttons.

Then one of the dark mouths seemed to
swell a bit and become more distinct, and I

thought I saw a violet mist come down. And I heard Polly scream. There was a *whooosh!* and I could swear I saw something whizz up the mist, something long and thin, wriggling like a fish.

Broops.

The dark hatch closed, the violet light shifted and went out. The sound made by the thing in the sky became high and urgent. I waited for a huge blast of power, roars and howls, shattering thrusts –

Nothing.

Suddenly, the sky was empty. Suddenly I was aware of bird song, the dawn chorus; and the idling motor of the journalist's car –

She had never switched it off; and her voice still saying, "I don't *believe* it, I don't *believe* it!" PC Fuzz Farmiloe was still there, looking at the sky, his mouth gaping. For that matter, the *sky* was still there, rapidly brightening, and filled with those small separate clouds that may mean a good day.

I ran indoors. Dad, in pyjamas, stood on the stairs looking sleepy and cross. He said, "What's up? I thought I heard something."

"Nothing, Dad, nothing."

"What's the time?"

"Morning, Dad."

He was too sleepy to notice all the gear I was carrying; and that I was fully dressed. "I'll bring you and Mum tea in half an hour, Dad. At quarter to eight."

He swallowed the lie, scratched, blinked and went back to bed.

Polly was kneeling by the fireplace in the living room, her cheeks wet with tears.

"There you are, see?" she said to me, accusingly. "You said it wouldn't happen, but it *did*. He's *gone*."

"Yes, I know."

Her face changed. Her lower lip stuck out. "I wish he was still here," she said. "I liked him."

"Yes, I know. So did I."

And now I'll tell you an amazing thing: *nobody believed me. Or their own eyes.*

I said to the journalist, "There! Wasn't it fantastic! And we've got it all on tape and film, the lot! We're rich! Famous!"

"I don't believe it" was all she said.

"What do you mean? You were there, you saw it! Or do you mean we won't be rich and famous?"

"Both," she said. "I don't believe either."

"But for goodness' sake!"

"Spaceships, UFOs, all that stuff," she said, "It's not wanted. Nobody will buy it."

"But you *saw* it, with your own eyes!"

"I don't believe what I saw," she said. "I don't want to believe it."

"But I can show you the viddy pictures I took!"

"Sorry, love. They'd only say I'm a nutter. You too."

"Hang on! PC Farmiloe saw it too!"

"Talk to him, love. I'm bushed."

I talked to him. I said the same things I'd said to the girl. He listened patiently. When I had finished, he reached in his pocket and said, "See this?"

"Yes. It's your notebook. You have to take notes."

"That's right. Well, now... See this?" He opened the notebook and showed me a blank page.

"That's my notes for this spell of duty," he told me.

"But there are no notes! It's empty!"

"That's right, son. Empty. And that's the way it stays."

I tracked down two or three more people who must have seen the spaceship. They didn't want to know. When I asked them what they had seen, it was as if I were accusing them of some crime.

I even got hold of the old man with the allotment. At last I had some success. "Oh, I saw 'im all right!" he said. "Couldn't hardly miss 'im, could you?"

"So you'll back me up!" I began.

He interrupted me. "'Course, you wasn't in the war, was you?" he said. "The last little show, the 39-45. I was, didn't get out till '46. Talk about bangs and wallops and bombs! That one last night was nothing! Land-mines, now, they dropped them hung on parachutes…"

Sometimes There...

"At least let's try," Polly said.

I said, "I'm not sure we should. Or that I want to."

"Oh, you only say that because he liked me best. And because you didn't get rich and famous. I think that was very vul-gah of you."

"I thought you were the one who wanted to be a pop star, with a Roller and everything."

"That's different," she sniffed. "And anyhow, I really can sing."

"Please don't."

"Well, at least we could *try*," she said.

"All right, you do it."

She switched the TV set on. Then off. Then on. Then off.

Nothing happened, of course. Yet Polly kept at it, she never gave up. As the weeks passed, I would often find her with the remote control in her hand, switching on and off, off and on.

"Broops!" she said. "Come on, Broops! It's me, Polly, your friend!"

I remember sniffing and leaving her to it on the day the sweep called to do our chimney. I remember how amazed he was; he'd never seen a chimney that clean, had we been up it with a pail and scrubbing brush, ha ha?

That made me think again of Broops, and how he looked, and how, really, I missed him, the great fat furry old thing. I was thinking about him really hard and Polly once again began playing with the remote control, on and off, off and on —

And there he was! On the screen! Wagging a big, woolly paw!

"Broops!" Polly shouted. "Oh, Broops!"

And we just had time, before the picture faded, to wave back at him – and to hear the word he spoke, which was "riddle".

Then Polly started all over again with the remote control, on and off, and Broops kept appearing and disappearing.

"Riddle!" Polly squeaked. "Go on about the riddle!"

"Why does the..." Broops managed to say, before he faded.

"Go on, I'm listening, go on!" Polly shouted, furiously pushing buttons to make Broops reappear.

"...chicken cross the..." Broops said, and vanished.

"...road?" Broops said, when he returned to the screen.

"Ooh! Oh! I know the answer, I do!" Polly yelled, bouncing up and down on her backside. "I do know it!"

I ask you, who doesn't know it! I left them at it. I mean, how corny can you get?

But I admit that sometimes, when I'm alone in the house, I press the buttons. And sometimes, not very often, Broops is there, just for a moment, and we wave and grin and pull stupid faces.

As I say, it does not happen very often.

But it is nice when it does.